A heartfelt appreciation to family and friends for their cheers of support,
the Wolfe "family" for endless patience and friendship,
the inspiring talent of Gavriel and Art, to Linda Stark for her selfless
generosity, and to the magical beauty that is the Southwest.

—A.H.

Text © 2002 by Andrea Helman
Photography © 2002 by Art Wolfe and Gavriel Jecan
All rights reserved.

www.northlandpub.com

Composed in the United States of America
Printed in Hong Kong

Text type was set in Gill Sans.
Display type was set in Latino.
Edited by Rebecca Gómez.
Editorial assistance by Rebekah Bereit.
Designed by Lanie Schwichtenberg.
Production supervised by Donna Boyd.

FIRST IMPRESSION

ISBN 0-87358-798-7

02 03 04 05 06   5 4 3 2 1

Library of Congress Cataloging-In-Publication Data Pending

C is for Coyote

Photographs by
Art Wolfe
and
Gavriel Jecan

Text by
Andrea Helman

C is for Coyote
A Southwest Alphabet Book

rising moon

A is for Arches

Delicate Arch stands alone surrounded by sculptured rock towers and domes that are more than 150 million years old. Ice, snow, rain, and wind will eventually destroy these natural works of wonder—and at the same time create new ones.

B is for Bobcat

Peering out from a rocky den, this bobcat
awaits the night, his favorite time to hunt.
A solitary animal, the bobcat may look
like a sweet pet, but is really quite fierce.
His g-r-o-w-l is very deep and scary.

is for Coyote

One of the most adaptable animals in the world, coyotes are very clever. Yip! Yip! Oo-oow! Known for their distinctive howl, some Native Americans call coyotes "songdogs" and interpret their howling to predict the weather.

D is for Dune

Like rippled white snow, huge mounds of sand form dunes at White Sands National Monument. The dunes are always on the move as strong winds blow the sparkly crystals up one side and w h o o s h ! down the other.

E is for Elk

Using a keen sense of smell to detect danger and long agile legs to run and jump, male elks call out like bugles when looking for a mate. They polish their five foot antlers on tree trunks and shed them after mating season.

F is for Flowers

Thousands of perennials, like these brightly colored asters, bloom year after year throughout the Southwest. The Navajo sometimes use the dried powdered plant to relieve headaches, toothaches, and sore eyes.

G

is for Grand Canyon

How did the Grand Canyon become so grand? It took five million years for the Colorado River to carve it, creating the largest and deepest canyon in North America. It's the eighth natural wonder of the world!

H is for Hummingbird

Slurp! The brightly colored Calliope hummingbird whizzes about searching for sweet nectar to eat. Only three inches long, the smallest bird in North America eats half its weight each day. For you that would mean 80 hamburgers…a day!

I is for Indian Ruin

Nestled below towering cliffs or perched high on ledges are the ruins of ancient villages. Rock art decorates the walls surrounding the cliff dwellings at White House Ruins, built by prehistoric Anasazi Indians.

J is for Javelina

You would probably smell these javelinas before seeing them. Their musky odor helps the nearsighted creatures locate other herd members. Javelinas eat fruit and nuts, but their favorite meal is prickly pear cactus. Ouch!

K is for Kestrel

Klee! Klee! Klee! This small colorful falcon makes up for its size with a piercing call. Sometimes called a sparrow hawk, the American kestrel has the clear facial markings of the falcon family— sideburns and a mustache.

L is for Lizard

Is that lizard doing push-ups? When in danger, some lizards can shed their tails to free themselves from an attacker. Within a month most lizards re-grow their tails, which help them climb, swim, and run.

M is for Mountain Lion

Mountain lions, found more in the Southwest than anywhere else in the United States, are strong and agile hunters. They can leap great distances, sometimes half the length of a basketball court!

N is for Native American

Tewa Deer Dancers move to the boom! boom! boom!
of drums at the San Ildefonso Pueblo Feast Day.
The dance, like a prayer, honors the animals they imitate.

O is for Owl

The tiny Elf owl spends its days safe from predators in a cozy cactus home drilled by a woodpecker. At night, the owl's excellent eyesight and hearing will lead it to a yummy meal of large insects.

P is for Pueblo

One thousand years ago, Pueblo Indians mixed water, straw, and earth (adobe) to create the Taos Pueblo, one of the oldest communities in the United States. In Spanish, "pueblo" means town.

Q is for Quail

The social Gambel's quail is widespread and well-adapted for the desert. Darting across the ground, this talkative bird chooses flight over fight. When disturbed, the flock rushes around in different directions, flapping their wings wildly to confuse any predators.

R is for Rattlesnake

"Back off!" warns a startled rattlesnake with the shake shake of its tail. Rattlers can't hear, so to find food they catch scents with their tongues or follow the ground vibrations of lizards and small animals.

S is for Saguaro

The Giant Saguaro, which is the largest cactus in the United States, can live up to 200 years and weigh as much as a small elephant! Growing up to 50 feet tall, the Saguaro produces a fragrant fruit and is home to more than a dozen species of birds, small mammals, and insects.

T is for Tarantula

This tarantula has eight eyes but uses sensitive leg hairs for guidance because it's almost blind! If food is scarce, tarantulas simply plug up their underground burrows and take a snooze for more than two years without food.

U
is for
Ultra-Violet Rays

Invisible ultra-violet (UV) rays are created by the sun, our nearest star. Even though the sun is 93 million miles away, these rays are harmful to your skin and eyes. So smooth on some sunscreen and slip on a pair of cool sunglasses.

V is for Vulture

Dark feathers absorb the sun's heat and warm the turkey vulture's body after a cool night. Awkward on land, this large bird of prey spreads its wings and soars effortlessly on the warm desert air in search of its next meal.

W is for Wolf

Does this Mexican Gray wolf look like a dog? That's because wolves are ancestors of dogs. Nearly extinct, the Mexican Gray wolf is an endangered species now being raised in captivity and released back into its wilderness home.

X is for San Xavier del Bac Mission

This bright adobe mission, which has survived earthquakes, floods, and war is called the "White Dove of the Desert." Filled with paintings, sculptures, and wall murals, the mission poses many mysteries. Who built it? Who were the artists? And, why was it left unfinished?

is for Yucca

Scattered throughout the Southwest deserts, the Soaptree Yucca is named for the soapy substance found inside its roots. The Yucca provides perches for hawks, tender flower stalks for hungry cattle and deer, and gentle soap for washing hand-woven rugs and blankets.

Z is for Zion

Look up! Zion National Park has some of the highest cliffs in America—2,000 feet from top to bottom. Zion is home to many mammals, birds, sandstone sculptures, and waterfalls.

ART WOLFE is one of the world's most acclaimed photographers, considered a master of composition and light. Based in Seattle, he travels the world shooting his outstanding images of wildlife and nature. His photographs appear in publications around the world, including *National Geographic, Smithsonian,* and *Outside.* He has published over forty books, including *The Living Wild, Africa,* and *The High Himalaya*, and nine books for children, including *Animal Action Alphabet,* and *Hiding Out.*

GAVRIEL JECAN began his photography career at the early age of 10. In 1994, he joined Art Wolfe, Inc. and has since then shared cover credit for photos in Wolfe's books *Colorado* and *Pacific Northwest: Land of Light and Water.* Jecan's images continue to appear regularly in major calendars and magazines worldwide, including *International Wildlife, National Wildlife Federation, Kids Discover, Outside,* and *National Geographic.* His latest work has been featured in international ad campaigns for Hasselblad.

ANDREA HELMAN is an award-winning freelance and television writer, producer, and talent. Her articles and humor essays have appeared in numerous regional and national publications, including *Redbook, The Christian Science Monitor, McCall's,* and *Left Bank.* Her four children's books include *O is for Orca,* and *Northwest Animal Babies.*